For my dad —BB

For Samuel —EB

ABOUT THIS BOOK

The illustrations for this book were done in pencil and watercolor. This book was edited by Andrea Spooner, art directed by David Caplan, and designed by Kelly Brennan. The production was supervised by Lillian Sun, and the production editor was Jen Graham. The text was set in Perpetua, and the display type is Strange Times.

THE Great Whipplethorp Bug Collection

Written by **Ben Brashares** • Illustrated by **Elizabeth Bergeland**

Little, Brown and Company

New York Boston

Summer days were long for Chuck Whipplethorp in his new house on Normal Street. He often went outside, where he felt the chances of something interesting happening were slightly better.

He was often wrong.

If all else failed, Chuck always had his dad to pester.

"Dad? I'm bored," Chuck said.

"Go build a fort. That's what I did when I was a kid," his dad replied.

"Or you could always help unpack some of these boxes...."

Chuck groaned. "I'm not *that* bored."

He watched his dad hunch over his computer, typing.

"Dad?" he asked. "Am I going to be as boring as you when I grow up?"

Chuck's dad couldn't help but laugh. "If you're lucky, Chuck."

It wasn't long before Chuck decided that

he was,

in fact,

bored enough

to unpack boxes.

"I remember this," Chuck said, as he unwrapped a glass case filled with brightly colored insects perfectly pinned to a board. "Grandpa made it, right?"

"That was his first bug collection. He made it when he was nine."

"*Nine?!*" Chuck gasped. *His* last science project had resulted in a pile of broken toothpicks and a marshmallow up his nose.

"Grandpa even discovered a whole new insect species when he got older," his dad added.

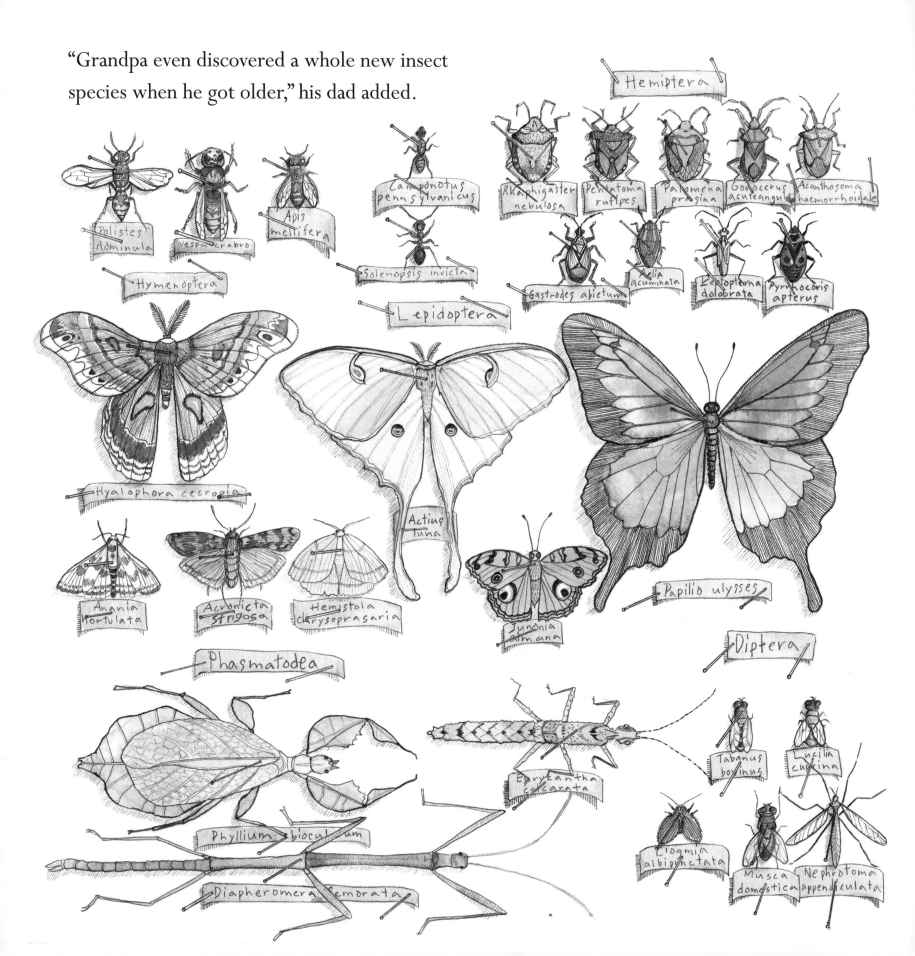

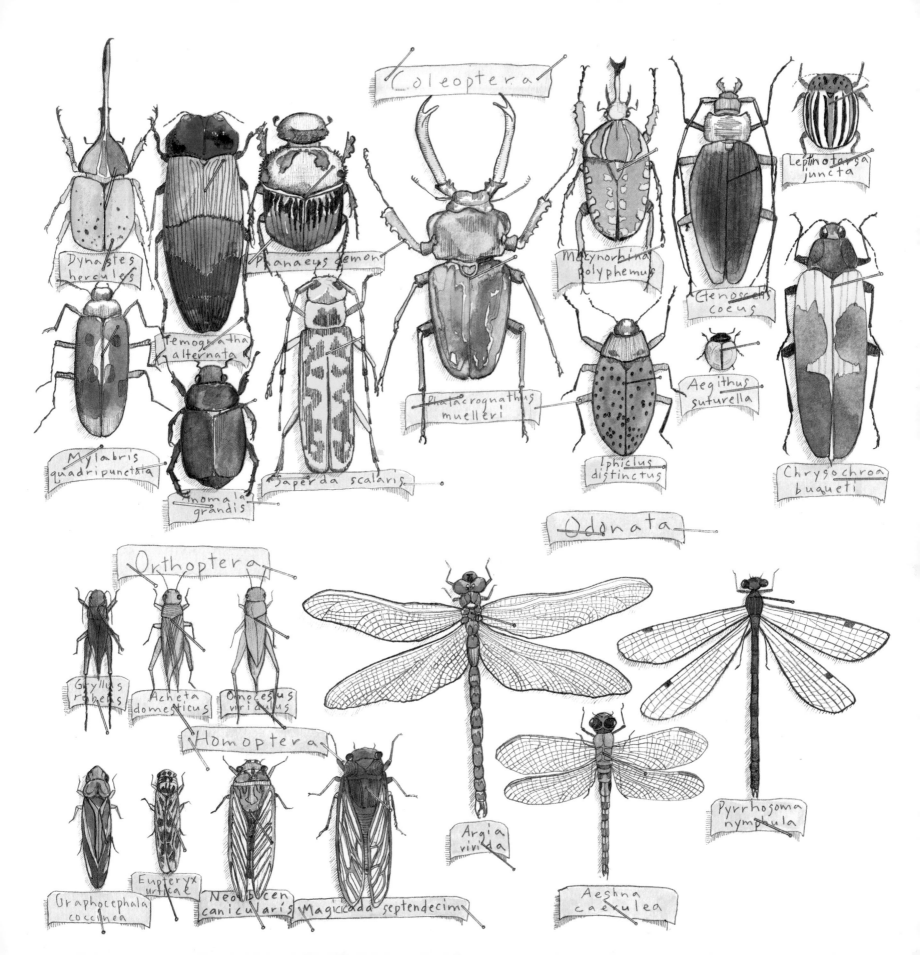

Coleoptera

Dynastes hercules

Temognatha alternata

Phanaeus demon

Mylabris quadripunctata

Anomala grandis

Saperda scalaris

Phalacrognathus muelleri

Mecynorhina polyphemus

Ctenoscelis coeus

Iphiclus distinctus

Aegithus suturella

Lepinotarsa juncta

Chrysochroa buqueti

Orthoptera

Gryllus rubens

Acheta domesticus

Onocestus viridius

Homoptera

Graphocephala coccinea

Eupteryx urticae

Neotibicen canicularis

Magicicada septendecim

Odonata

Argia vivida

Aeshna caerulea

Pyrrhosoma nymphula

That night, Chuck had trouble concentrating on his bedtime story.

"I can't believe Grandpa really made that bug collection when he was a kid.

His dad must have helped him, right?" Chuck asked.

"Nope. His dad, your great-grandpa, was mostly gone, sailing around the world.

He was a deep-sea diver."

"Really?"

"He actually got attacked by an octopus once. And *his* dad, your great-great-grandfather, was gone even more, fighting in wars and climbing mountains.

He once lost three toes to frostbite on Mount Everest."

"Seriously?" Chuck had no idea his ancestors were so cool.

His dad put the book down and told Chuck all about
the great Whipplethorp men before him.

CHARLES VAN VELSOR WHIPPLETHORP I

Decorated Soldier, Mountain Climber

CHARLES VAN VELSOR WHIPPLETHORP II

Navy Admiral, Oceanographer

CHARLES VAN VELSOR WHIPPLETHORP III

Famed Entomologist, World Traveler

CHARLIE WHIPPLETHORP

Dad, Data Analyst, Amusement Park Enthusiast

Chuck was concerned.

The great Whipplethorp men, it appeared, were getting…a lot less great.

"Big plans today, Chuckster?"
"It's *Charles*. Yes, very big plans."

The tallest peak on Normal Street—a large pile of mulch—offered little chance of frostbitten toes. So Chuck moved on to the second adventure on his list.

"Mom? Which way is the ocean from here?"

"About fifteen hundred miles east.
Or west."

On to number three.
Finding a new species, Chuck determined,
had to be easier.

"It looks like it's a…Yup!" his dad exclaimed. "It's a wood-boring beetle!"

"So it isn't new?" Chuck sighed. "And it's even called a *boring* beetle?"

"*Wood*-boring beetle," his dad said. "And just because it isn't a new species doesn't mean it isn't super cool. Maybe it's the first insect in your own great collection."

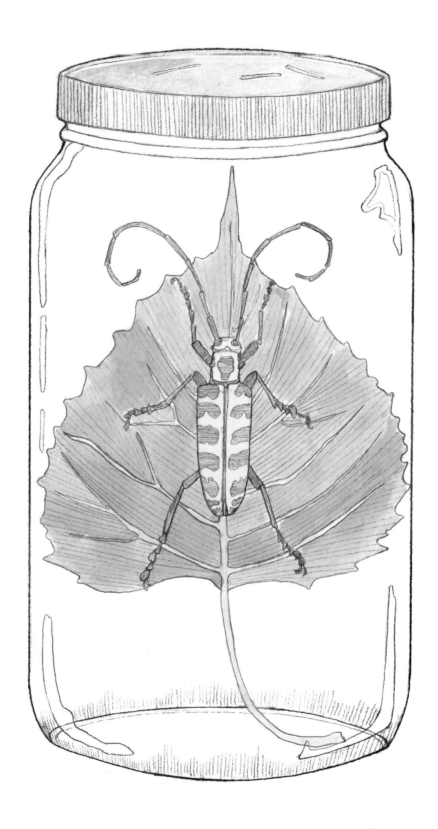

One even better than Grandpa's, Chuck thought. To start, all he had to do was...

...kill

...one

...small

...beetle.

New plan: Collect insects that are already dead.

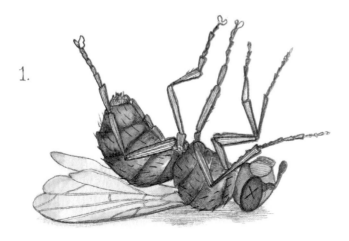

1.

Musca domestica
LOCATION: WINDOWSILL
CAUSE OF DEATH: NATURAL CAUSES

2.

Musca domestica
LOCATION: LAMP
CAUSE OF DEATH: NATURAL CAUSES

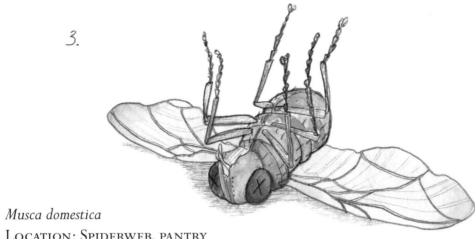

3.

Musca domestica
LOCATION: SPIDERWEB, PANTRY
CAUSE OF DEATH: GUTS EATEN

"Well," Chuck's dad said, staring at the collection, "it's different from Grandpa's."

Chuck grumbled. "Different means bad."

"Not at all." Chuck's dad looked at Chuck. "You didn't want to hurt your beetle, and you made something new because of that. That's how things change. That's how they get better."

Chuck didn't think his dead-fly collection was a change for the better. But as he watched his boring beetle crawl around a tiny jar, he had an idea for something that *could* be.

Maybe even something great.

"Has anyone seen my charge cord?…
Chuuuuck!"

"Who put the milk back
without the cap? And why
does NOTHING in the
fridge have its lid?!
…*Chuuuuck!*"

"Where are the CAR KEYS?!?
Chuuuuuck??"

Outside, Chuck found just the right spot and gently placed his beetle inside its new home. "I hope you like it," he said. "And you can invite other bugs, too. Okay? Good night."

"Wow, Chuck," his dad said the next morning. "It's like a bug collection but for live, happy bugs."

"I put a lollipop in there to get more to come," Chuck explained.

"I think it worked." Chuck's dad leaned in for a closer look.

"And, wow, look at that…the cap to the milk…and…the car keys!? Seriously?" His dad shook his head and laughed. "It's great, Chuck. You should be really proud."

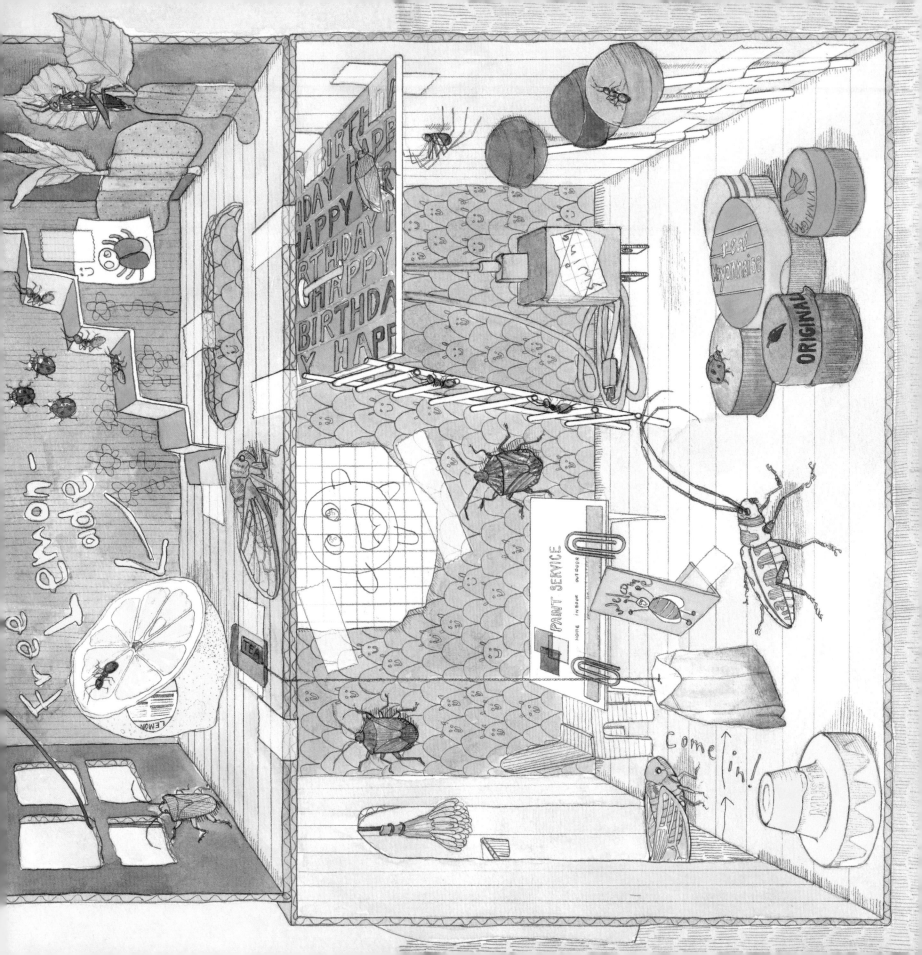

At bedtime, Chuck thought more about his grand and great ancestors as
he climbed under the covers. "Dad," he said, "I'm kinda glad you're boring.
It means you're around a lot."
"Around a lot with *you*," Chuck's dad added. "That's the adventure *I* always wanted."
"That's still kind of a boring adventure, Dad."
Chuck's dad laughed. "It's a lot like wrestling an octopus, actually," he said as
he wrapped his arms around Chuck and tickled him.

Then, as they began reading, Chuck had an interesting
thought: Maybe the Whipplethorp men weren't getting
worse. Maybe they were just getting…different. And
that's how things change. That's how they get better.